This book belongs to

Jamie
Atwell

Little Red Riding Hood

BARRON'S
New York. Toronto

Once upon a time, there was a girl called Little Red Riding Hood because she always wore her favorite red coat with a hood that her grandmother had made for her. One day, her mother asked her to take a basket of goodies to her grandmother, who was not feeling well.

"Hurry along," her mother said, "and don't talk to strangers."

Little Red Riding Hood promised and off she ran. She skipped along the path, singing as she went.

Little Red Riding Hood stopped to pick some flowers.
Suddenly, there appeared a big, bad wolf! The wolf asked
her where she was going with her basket of goodies. She
replied, ''I'm taking some cakes and homemade cider to

my grandmother, who is not feeling well. She lives on the other side of the forest.''

"Well," said the wolf, "I'm going to that side of the forest myself, but I'm afraid I'm late. Good day!"

With a swish of his bushy tail, the wolf was gone. He knew where Little Red Riding Hood's grandmother lived, and he knew a quicker path. He raced off ahead of Little Red Riding Hood. Meanwhile, she was enjoying her walk. She picked more flowers, and sat down to eat a cake and drink some of the cider that her mother had packed for her in the basket.

The wolf arrived at Grandmother's house in no time. He knocked at the door. Grandmother got up to answer the door, but first she looked out of the window. She was shocked to see a big wolf. She ran out of the back door.

The wolf opened the door and, finding no one home,
decided to put on Grandmother's nightgown and pretend
to be Grandmother when Little Red Riding Hood
arrived.

After he had pulled the blankets up over his chin, he heard a knock at the door.

"Hello, Grandmother, it's me, Little Red Riding Hood!" she called.

"Come in, dear, the door isn't locked," said the wolf softly.

"I've brought you some cake and cider from Mother," said Little Red Riding Hood, shutting the door behind her.

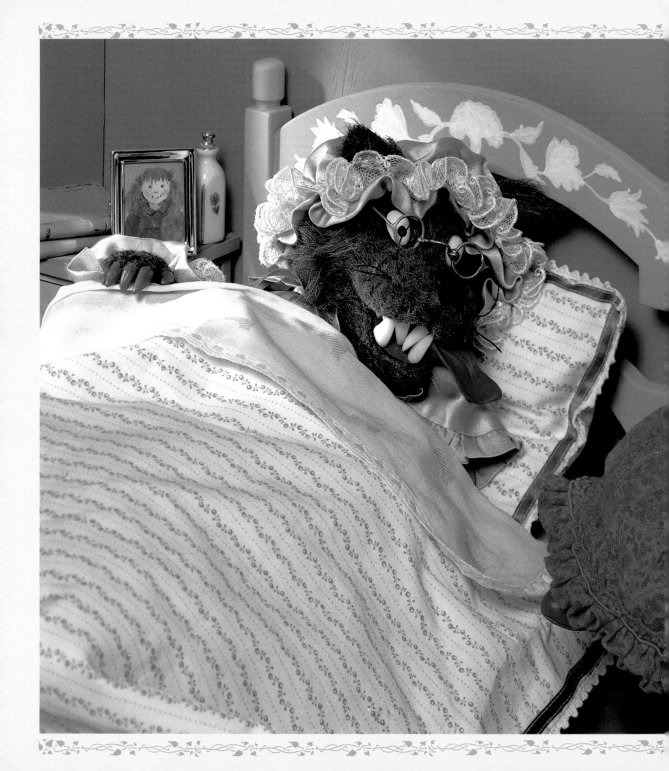

"Why, Grandmother," exclaimed Little Red Riding Hood, as she sat by the wolf, "what big eyes you have!"

"All the better to see you with, my dear," said the wolf.

"And Grandmother, what big ears you have!"

"All the better to hear you with, my dear," replied the wolf.

"Grandmother, what big teeth you have!" cried Little Red Riding Hood.

"The better to eat you with!" said the wolf, jumping up. He leapt out of bed, toward Little Red Riding Hood.

Just then, Grandmother rushed in with a hunter. The hunter shot the wicked wolf, just as he was trying to escape out of the window. Little Red Riding Hood ran toward Grandmother and they hugged each other happily.

They thanked the hunter over and over. Then they invited him to stay and have some cake and cider. He readily agreed. As it turned out, the hunter had been looking for the wolf for a long time.

The three of them went into the kitchen and had a little party. Little Red Riding Hood told the hunter that she had learned a very valuable lesson that day. Never again would she talk to strangers anywhere!